To Maudie, with a massive FIZZ, WHIZZ, POP!

– J L

LITTLE TIGER PRESS LTD
an imprint of the Little Tiger Group
1 Coda Studios, 189 Munster Road, London SW6 6AW
www.littletiger.co.uk

First published in Great Britain 2018

A CIP catalogue record for this book is available from the British Library

 • ISBN 978-1-84869-821-5

Printed in China • LTP/1400/1979/0817

Jonny Lambert

LOOK OUT, It's a Dragon!

LITTLE TIGER
LONDON

Saffi wasn't like other dragons.

She didn't want to crush castles

or capture princesses.

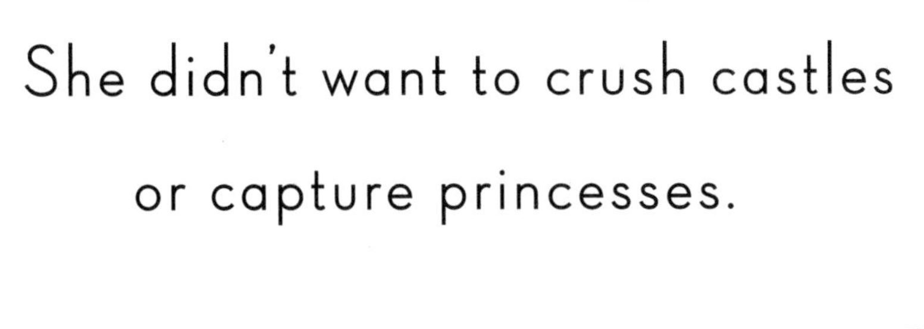

And sitting on cold, rocky

mountains just hurt her bottom.

"That's it," said Saffi. "I'm off!"

She searched far and wide until she found . . .

. . . a sunny, woodland home.

"Hello, neighbours," beamed Saffi, landing

KERUMPH in a field full of flowers.

"Argh! It's a dragon!" cried the forest animals.

"Run away!"

"Don't go!
It's wonderful here,"
Saffi sighed happily,
wriggling in the
long, soft grass.

But from behind her, a little voice squeaked,

"Oi!
Knobbly knickers!
You can't stay here!"

“But I love it,” replied Saffi. “Why can’t I stay?”

“Because you’re a **dragon!**” Mouse exclaimed. “We know what dragons do. They chase us with their fiery flames.”

"Not me," said Saffi.
"I'm a friendly dragon. **Look!"**

And she collected Mouse
a clutch of corn for his tea.

"Thank you," squeaked Mouse,
a little surprised.

But just then, Saffi's nose began to itch . . .

"AAAATISHOOO!"

Saffi sneezed an **enormous** sneeze and accidentally sizzled Warbler's tail.

"Eek!"
squeaked Mouse.

"Argh!"

cried Warbler.

"I've been scorched by a **dragon** . . .

And now it's coming after me!"

Saffi swooped after the songbird.

"Please come back. You've got it wrong –
I just want to be your friend!"

But Warbler didn't stop.

And Saffi followed her . . .

CRASH!

SMASH!

SPLINTER!

. . . toppling birds from their treetops.

"Argh!" cried the animals. "A dragon is squashing our homes!"

Enough was enough.

"STOP, you lumbering beastie!"

bellowed Mouse. "You can't live here.

Leave us all alone."

Saffi's ears drooped and she plodded away.

"It really was a lovely home,"

she sniffed sadly.

"Good riddance!" muttered Mouse,
and the animals snuggled down for a snooze.

But as they slept,
eerie shadows crept.

Closer and larger, the shadows loomed. Then . . .

FIZZLE!
SCORCH!
SINGE!

The animals scattered this way and that,

chased by **fiery, scary dragons!**

"Help!" they cried.

"Somebody help us!"

And somebody did!

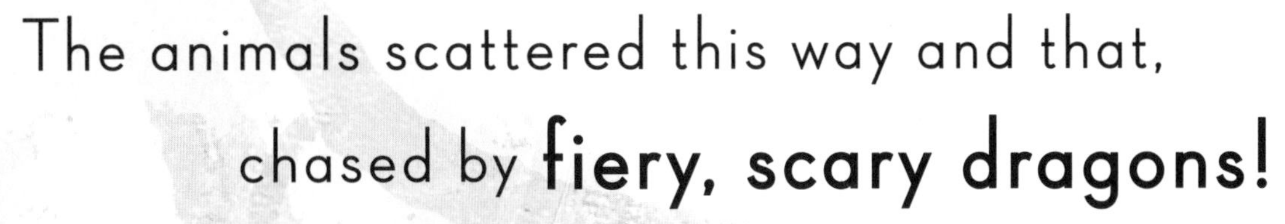

Whoosh!

"Nobody hurts my friends!" cried Saffi, swooping in and chasing off the dragons.

"Thank you, Saffi!" the animals cheered. "We're sorry we told you to leave."

But the woodland was scorched
and the trees no more.
"We can't stay here,"
said Mouse.

So Saffi took off and searched far and wide
until she found . . .

. . . a happy, new home for them all!

"**It's perfect!**" cried the animals.

And it was.

There was sunshine and flowers, and space for everyone, even the biggest of friends.